For my dad who never forgot to show kindness and love to everyone he knew.

- Corinne

For my Grammie who showed unconditional empathy to all.

- Jessica

Look for the silhouettes of the state of Virginia throughout the book!

www.mascotbooks.com

Winter's Warmth

Railcam photo courtesy of Virtual Railfan.

For more information, please contact:
Mascot Books
620 Herndon Parkway #320
Herndon, VA 20170
info@mascotbooks.com

Library of Congress Control Number: 2019908269

CPSIA Code: PRT0819A
ISBN-13: 978-1-64543-098-8

Printed in the United States

Winter's Warmth

Share the warmth! ♡ Corinne Luck

Written by **Corinne Luck**

Illustrated by **Jessica Bruce**

In a sweet little town
On a cold wintery day,
Near the trackside
Two girls went to play.

The snow gently fell
And covered the ground.
There was suddenly white
Where once there was brown.

A red bird watched
As the scene came alive.
More cardinals joined in
With a flutter, swoop, and dive.

Those snowmen in town
Were simple and sweet,
Leaving happy people and hearts
All along the main street.

The town loved the snowmen
And the animals did, too.
In the harsh winter weather
They knew just what they'd do.

Gray squirrel gazed
Into one snowman's eyes.
He knew that those acorns
Were hard to deny.

Up upon the next one
Hopped the cottontail bunny.
He munched on her nose,
Filling his tummy.

The white-tailed deer chewed the twigs
Until the snowmen went down.
The sweet postcard scene
Was now a mess on the ground.

At sunrise the next day,
All the glee disappeared.
Who'd do such a thing?
Then a cardinal appeared!

The kids started thinking,
And after seeing a need,
They quickly dashed off
To collect twigs, nuts, and seeds.

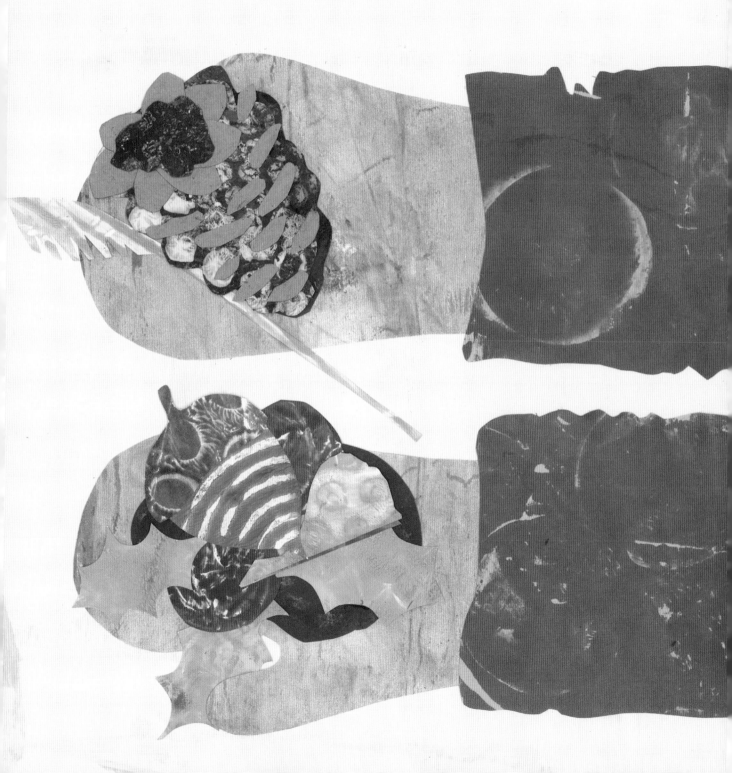

Rebuilding the snowmen
Was the right thing to do.
That beautiful cardinal
Was a crystal clear clue.

The fun in the snow
For those two little girls
Became a wintertime feast
For the deer, bunny, and squirrels.

Building new snowmen
Upon the same ground;
Now there's plenty to eat
For every animal around.

As daytime ended
And the sun went down,
Echoes of full hearts were left
In the small railroad town.

The three snowmen as captured by the railcam.

Corinne and Jessica discovered friendship and dreams at a small preschool in Ashland, Virginia. Corinne has worked in early childhood education for 26 years, and Jessica has worked in art education for nine years, but they've only worked together for the past year. The two paired up to bring their first children's book to life after seeing a photo of three snowmen captured by a public railcam in their tiny town in December 2018. The photo inspired Corinne's story, and Jessica brought that story to life by collage and mixed media using handmade printed paper.

Corinne and Jessica hope *Winter's Warmth* reminds everyone to be generous, celebrate their blessings, and fill up their hearts by spreading goodness and gratitude always.

Discover the original video of the inspiration for this story on YouTube: https://youtu.be/tb3UZsWQo6Y